For Olivia & Julia, :)
Happy Hopping!
Susan Jolliffe

P9-DEM-677

The Twelve Days of Summer

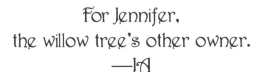

For Jennifer,
the willow tree's other owner.
—JA

To Bill, Keltie, Tom, the Walking Women
and all the Little River Creatures
—SRJ

Text copyright © 2005 Jan Andrews

Illustrations copyright © 2005 Susan Rennick Jolliffe

All rights reserved. No part of this publication may be reproduced or transmitted in
any form or by any means, electronic or mechanical, including photocopying, recording
or by any information storage and retrieval system now known or to be invented, without
permission in writing from the publisher.

National Library of Canada Cataloguing in Publication Data:

Andrews, Jan, 1942-

The twelve days of summer / story by Jan Andrews;
illustrations by Susan Rennick Jolliffe.

ISBN 1-55143-365-6

I. Jolliffe, Susan II. Title.

PS8551.N37T83 2005   jC813'.54   C2004-906756-7

First published in the United States 2005

Library of Congress Control Number: 2004116125

Summary: In this counting book that celebrates summer and the cycle of life,
a child finds creative ways to interact with the creatures in a beautiful garden.

Orca Book Publishers gratefully acknowledges the support for its publishing
programs provided by the following agencies: the Government of Canada through
the Book Publishing Industry Development Program (BPIDP), the Canada Council
for the Arts, and the British Columbia Arts Council.

Design by Lynn O'Rourke
Printed and bound in Hong Kong

Orca Book Publishers
Box 5626 Stn. B
Victoria, BC Canada
V8R 6S4

Orca Book Publishers
PO Box 468
Custer, WA   USA
98240-0468

08 07 06 05 ◆ 4 3 2 1

The Twelve Days
of Summer

story by Jan Andrews

illustrations by Susan Rennick Jolliffe

ORCA BOOK PUBLISHERS

On my first day of summer,
the sunshine brought to me

A song sparrow nest
for three.

On my second day of summer,
the sunshine brought to me

Two goatsbeard seeds

And a song sparrow nest
for three.

On my third day of summer,
the sunshine brought to me

Three ruffed grouse

Two goatsbeard seeds

And a song sparrow nest
for three.

On my fourth day of summer,
    the sunshine brought to me

Four garter snakes

Three ruffed grouse

Two goatsbeard seeds

And a song sparrow nest
            for three.

On my fifth day of summer,
the sunshine brought to me

Five bumble bees

Four garter snakes

Three ruffed grouse

Two goatsbeard seeds

And a song sparrow nest
for three.

HONEY

On my sixth day of summer,
  the sunshine brought to me

Six hawks a-soaring

Five bumble bees

Four garter snakes

Three ruffed grouse

Two goatsbeard seeds

And a song sparrow nest
          for three.

On my seventh day of summer,
    the sunshine brought to me

Seven moles a-digging

Six hawks a-soaring

Five bumble bees

Four garter snakes

Three ruffed grouse

Two goatsbeard seeds

And a song sparrow
        nest for three.

On my eighth day of summer,
the sunshine brought to me

Eight toads a-hopping

Seven moles a-digging

Six hawks a-soaring

Five bumble bees

Four garter snakes

Three ruffed grouse

Two goatsbeard seeds

And a song sparrow
nest for three.

toad house

On my ninth day of summer,
  the sunshine brought to me

Nine daisies dancing

Eight toads a-hopping

Seven moles a-digging

Six hawks a-soaring

Five bumble bees

Four garter snakes

Three ruffed grouse

Two goatsbeard seeds

And a song sparrow nest
      for three.

On my tenth day of summer,
  the sunshine brought to me

Ten crows a-cawing

Nine daisies dancing

Eight toads a-hopping

Seven moles a-digging

Six hawks a-soaring

Five bumble bees

Four garter snakes

Three ruffed grouse

Two goatsbeard seeds

And a song sparrow nest
              for three.

On my eleventh day of summer,
the sunshine brought to me

Eleven swallows gliding

Ten crows a-cawing

Nine daisies dancing

Eight toads a-hopping

Seven moles a-digging

Six hawks a-soaring

Five bumble bees

Four garter snakes

Three ruffed grouse

Two goatsbeard seeds

And a song sparrow nest
for three.

On my twelfth day of summer,
the sunshine brought to me

Twelve eggs a-hatching

Eleven swallows gliding

Ten crows a-cawing

Nine daisies dancing

Eight toads a-hopping

Seven moles a-digging

Six hawks a-soaring

Five bumble bees

Four garter snakes

Three ruffed grouse

Two goatsbeard seeds

And a song sparrow
nest for three.

FACTS — COMMON AND CURIOUS

DAY 1   Watch out for the male song sparrow. He'll be on the top of a tree or a bush or a post, tilting his head back, opening his beak and letting out a series of notes that end on a long trill.

DAY 2   Most flowers open wider as the day goes on, but the goatsbeard closes its petals when the sun is brightest. That's why the plant's other name is Johnny-go-to-bed-at-noon.

DAY 3   If you hear drumming in the woods in spring time it's probably a male ruffed grouse. He's cupping his wings and beating them extra fast in an effort to attract a mate.

DAY 4   The moneywort vine the snake is resting on in the picture was once known as serpentaria. That's because people believed that snakes would lie on it to heal their wounds.

DAY 5   Bumblebees can gather honey when the weather is too cold for most other insects to fly. The bees keep themselves warm by shivering—just like we do.

DAY 6   Hawks soar when they're hunting. They can see eight times as well as humans, spot a mouse when it's thirty meters away and dive from the sky at speeds of almost two hundred kilometers an hour.

DAY 7   Moles live most of their lives under ground. Their fur is very soft and does not lie flat in any direction. This means they can move backwards or forwards with ease through tunnels that are not much bigger than they are.

DAY 8   If you see a toad, don't try to pick it up. Your hands will warm it, and toads need to stay cool. That's why they prefer to keep hidden during the day and to hunt for their food at night.

DAY 9   Ox-eye daisies like these were once used to make medicines to cure asthma, whooping cough, bruises and other ills. Ox-eyes are also called butter daisies because when cows eat them the milk and butter taste bad.

DAY 10   Crows like to play. They tumble and frolic in the skies. They play drop-and-catch on their own; they play tug of war with each other. They balance on flimsy perches and hang upside down for fun.

DAY 11   What do swallows do all day? They eat. Mostly they eat insects. They fly through the sky catching mosquitoes. Without them, we'd be scratching even more than we are now.

DAY 12   What's going to happen next? The young birds will grow up and fly away. The bigger birds will not lay any more eggs this summer. The song sparrows and the smaller birds will start all over again, perhaps in the same nests, perhaps in new ones. They will have more eggs a-hatching this same year.